Andrew Bell

General James Wolfe, his Life and Death

SALZWASSER
VERLAG

Andrew Bell

General James Wolfe, his Life and Death

Reprint of the original, first published in 1859.

1st Edition 2022 | ISBN: 978-3-37512-184-6

Verlag (Publisher): Salzwasser Verlag GmbH, Zeilweg 44, 60439 Frankfurt, Deutschland
Vertretungsberechtigt (Authorized to represent): E. Roepke, Zeilweg 44, 60439 Frankfurt, Deutschland
Druck (Print): Books on Demand GmbH, In de Tarpen 42, 22848 Norderstedt, Deutschland

BRITISH-CANADIAN CENTENNIUM,
1759 - 1859.

GENERAL JAMES WOLFE,
HIS LIFE AND DEATH:

A Lecture,

DELIVERED IN THE

MECHANICS' INSTITUTE HALL, MONTREAL,

ON TUESDAY, SEPTEMBER 13, 1859,

BEING

The Anniversary Day of the Battle of Quebec,

FOUGHT A CENTURY BEFORE,

IN WHICH BRITAIN LOST A HERO AND WON A PROVINCE.

BY ANDREW BELL,

Author of " Men and Things in America"; " Historical Sketches of Feudalism, British
and Continental"; " Lives of the Illustrious"; " New Annals of Old Scotland"; &c.

Montreal :
PRINTED AND PUBLISHED BY JOHN LOVELL,
ST. NICHOLAS STREET;
QUEBEC : STE. ANNE STREET, UPPER TOWN,
AND FOR SALE AT THE BOOK STORES.

1859.

[Price 25 Cents.

CENTENARY LECTURE

ON THE

LIFE OF GENERAL WOLFE,

AND

THE CONQUEST OF CANADA.

I NEED not remind you, my fellow-countryfolks and others, now met in this Hall, that just one hundred of the most eventful years known to metropolitan or colonial Britain, have revolved since the ever-memorable battle of the Plains of Abraham took place. Thinking, a year ago, that the recurrence of such a notable cycle in the course of time ought not to pass unheeded by the populations upon this continent whom it most concerned, and having been all but disappointed in my expectation, I determined that, in my personal capacity at least, I would make a further attempt to prove to the few within the sound of my feeble voice, as to those lately within the limited reach of my pen, that it was a fit occasion for a demonstration of intermingled sympathy, first in grateful memory of our British forefathers who triumphed, next of participation in the regrets of the race they vanquished; all which might be turned to profitable account, by soothing rather than irritating every alien feeling in the country of my adoption. An individual attempt at such a conciliation of our two races having failed, as I shall explain by and by, yet in order that the day should not pass quite unobserved, I have hastily penned the discourse I am about to utter.

To enable its hearers, and future readers, to estimate my
competence for taking up the subject now in hand, it may be
convenient to mention at the outset, that a few years ago, I was
one of a literary corps in London, engaged in bringing out a
biographical collection entitled "Lives of the Illustrious."*
Amongst the memoirs of eminent men, assigned to my care, was
that of General Wolfe. This was really to me, in prospect, a labour of love; but when I came to gather and arrange the needful
materials, I was literally dismayed at their scantiness. Except
the brief memorials given, during nearly a hundred years, in the
Biographica Britannica and Encyclopedias—all servilely copying
each other—and a few fugitive notices in the Annual Registers
and petty Magazines, obtained after weeks of unwearied research
at the British Museum and other repositories of books and MSS.,
public and private, I had not wherewith to build up a literary
memorial worthy of the subject, or anything at all likely to be
even moderately satisfactory to our public. No Life, in fact, properly speaking, yet exists, strangely enough! of either of two
great warriors, who strove heroically, these hundred years ago, the
one to preserve, the other to gain, each for his beloved fatherland
the guidance of the destinies of this, now the greatest colony
earth knows or ever has known. I need hardly add that I mean
no less the truly illustrious Marquis de Montcalm, than General
Wolfe.

The latter of these undying names, in fact, soared at once
from comparative obscurity into the highest sphere of military
renown; and contemporaries scarcely had time to mark the
ascension of his "bright particular star" ere the corporeal being
over whom it culminated, was suddenly and for ever lost to
visual observation. As his mortal remains were embalmed
indeed, and reposited in that native soil which his great deeds and
greater aspirings illustrated; even so did his memory become a
sacred thing in his country's heart of hearts; but these duties

* The appearance of this collection, published during 1852-4, suddenly ceased when the publishers (Partridge & Oakey,) became bankrupt,
and it has not been resumed since.

once paid to the surpassing merits of Britain's "juvenile hero," scarcely one retroverted glance seems to have been cast, by the memorialists of the time, towards the personal or family antecedents of the man; an unworthy negligence which was noted and lamented by the late Robert Southey, obliging that eminent recorder of great actions to give up a meditated intention of writing his life, in utter despair of obtaining sufficient staple for the work.

Through favor of a happy chance, there was put into my humbler hands, by a friend, (James Buchanan, Esq., Glasgow, once, perhaps still, secretary of the Western Bank of Scotland), about the time mentioned, a packet containing thirteen original letters from Wolfe, written from various parts of North and South Britain, between the years 1749 and 1758. Twelve of these were addressed to Lieut. Colonel William Rickson, quarter-master general of the royal forces in Scotland; who seems to have been a brother in heart and mind, if not by blood, to his correspondent. In these letters I found many valuable notices of the military history of the time, as well as a few precious particulars of the writer's private life, and estimations of men and things around him.

Another likely source whence to obtain original information regarding my subject, and suggested by the gentleman who lent me the letter packet referred to, was that offered by the aids to historical inquiry lent in the London *Notes and Queries*. To the editor of that useful medium, therefore, I transmitted a call upon such of his correspondents as could furnish any unpublished notices, great or small, regarding the history, public and private, of General Wolfe. *Six* replies, each contributing interesting particulars, resulted. The helps thus derived, along with the unedited letters, and the material to be found in the best accredited biographies of the hero, enabled me to give to the British public if not a complete, yet a more satisfactory memorial of him at least, than had till then appeared.

The following were its opening passages :—

" Our military annals, during the eighteenth century, had much of an inglorious character. They began, indeed, with the triumph of a Marlborough, but they comprised the blunderings of Generals who were usually if not constantly beaten or outmanœuvred by the French marshals even of the olden *régime*, and they finished with the discomfiture of the Duke of York and his rabble-in-nniform at the Helder and elsewhere. Then there were the inglorious defeats of the Copes, the Hawleys, and the Wades, by handfuls of half-armed Highlanders, which marked the middle period of the Georgian age, to the astonishment of the world past and present. As for the dogged battlings of the pigtail-and-powder brigades set to work in Germany and Flanders, year after year, ' never ending still beginning,'—all for paltry personal interests too, of the two first Hanoverian rather than English Monarchs—while they added much to the debt of Britain, not a little detracted from its credit as a warlike nation. The contemporaneous battles, again, won or lost, by regular forces pitted against banded rebels, did little for our martial respectability in the estimation of mankind : for even the victor in civil war ought to be accorded rather a wreath of nightshade than a crown of laurel. In a word, almost the only bright page of the nearly barren military *fasti* in the last age, was that which blazons the conquest of Canada, begun and virtually consummated in one memorable day, the morning sun of which rose upon what was *Nouvelle France*, and set upon it as an added province of New England. High, indeed, was the cost of the prize then gained, for Providence had fixed its price at no less a rate than a fatal outpouring of the young life-blood of the heroic Wolfe."

Having thus had my attention turned as it were fortuitously to a subject ever the most interesting to a British patriot, it may 'well be supposed that, within a few hours of first setting my foot upon Canadian soil, I repaired to pay my heart's devoirs at the foot of the monumental memorial of Wolfe on the Plains of Abraham. And when, as editor of the *Montreal Pilot*, it was usual with me to note the recurrence of the anniversaries of remarkable national events, upon the evening of last Sept. 13 the following editorial, prefacing a short memoir of the hero, appeared in that newspaper :—

"HOMAGE TO THE ILLUSTRIOUS DEAD.—This day, ninety-nine years ago, was fought on the Plains of Abraham, that battle which caused Canada to pass from the domination of France to the rule of Great Britain. Will it be thought premature if we suggest now, that so great an event is all-worthy of a public CENTENNIAL CELEBRATION, if only to do honor to the memory of the two heroic paladins, sons of contending nations, whose precious life-blood was shed on the ever-memorable thirteenth day of September, 1759?"

The idea was favourably, in a few instances warmly, taken up by several members of the British Canadian press ; and it had a yet heartier response from sundry American journalists, those of Portland (Maine) especially, one of the latter claiming, that it should be made an "International Celebration." The proposal, however, met with a very different reception from the Gallo-Canadian press, the writers in which denounced, mocked, or carped at it, in the most bitter, nay even insulting terms. Never did a kindly meant and conciliatorily expressed "notion" meet more unworthy treatment than mine, from all my French confrères of Lower Canada. I was a little vexed at this, I must own, and not a little surprised ; for I had lived long in the mother country of these gentlemen, and where, such is my intimate knowledge of the character of the French people, a "demonstration" like that I proposed would have met general approval, perhaps even been hailed with enthusiasm. Thus, upon occasion of the disinterment, no further back than the year 1854, of the remains of those killed in that bootless fight which French Canadians call the "second battle, (and victory over the British!) of the Plains of Abraham," one of the leading and best journals of France, or of any other country, gave unqualified praise to that celebration, meant as it supposed (mistakingly it seems, however,) to do *equal* honor to the brave, fortunate and unfortunate, for the very deeds which I, in my simplicity, wished only *further* to do due reverence to; yet, for the time, I became the "best abused" editor in Canada, by all the journalists, whether ministerial or opposition, of the French-Canadian press.*

---

* See Supplement, B.

8

As no good ever came yet of returning railing for railing, I determined not to retaliate, further than by the following "retort courteous" in return for the bitterly inimical sentiments which were called up on the occasion in the over-sensitive Lower Canadian bosom, both against my fatherland and humble self:—

TRI-NATIONAL CENTENNIUM IN PROSPECT.—"We are glad to find that the suggestion we lately threw out, of the propriety of holding a centenarian celebration of the Battle of Quebec, 99 years ago, has been taken up, both in Canada and America. The Plains of Abraham became, after the 13th day of September, 1759, for ever sacred; for *there* was shed the life-blood of two of the most heroic spirits that ever inhabited human clay. Honour, never-dying honour, to the memory of Wolfe and Montcalm! When the deputed representatives of the three nations meet, as we trust they will, let the bleak battle-field of other days, now smiling under cultivation, be further consecrated by interchanging pledges of abiding amity between the men of the three nations who now worthily occupy one Continent of America, and who shall yet, if they do not virtually already, guide the destinies of the other.

"We confidently hope that the proposed celebration will not miscarry, through national or sectional jealousies between the living men of the two races, the descendants of those who gained, and of those who lost the day. We hope that *Jean Baptiste* is like *John Bull*, a respecter of a worthy foe, even when obliged to succumb. We will not wrong our Gallic fellow-subjects of this great and expanding Colony—the nucleus of an empire—by supposing that a majority of them bear any feeling but those of good-will and cordial emulation for their neighbours of British blood. We would fain believe, at least, that the petty self-dishonouring retorted taunts, occasionally appearing in the discourses, written and spoken, of partisan journals and orators, such as allusions to "les races supérieure et inférieure," (*proh pudor!*) are manifestive of surviving rabid inimity in the breasts of the few only. Yet has it been a cause of pain to the writer of the present sentences to note such things during his short experience here as a journalist, as fearing that, to use Lord Bacon's illustration of the occasional import of things infinitesimal, 'such as a straw, a light matter in itself, yea contemptible, it may yet serve to show what way the wind blows.'

"It is a common belief in Britain, well or ill founded, that Canada, as a Colony, is the petted, nay *spoiled*, child of the mother country. Without quite admitting this, we would, with all deference to Franco-Canadian opinions in that regard, ask them to concede this much to us That British domination has, in a general way, sat lightly upon the (so-called) "subjected" race. There is a proverb, in the predominant country, the sentiment of which, albeit too familiarly expressed, carries both wisdom and consolation in it. It runs thus :—' When two men ride the same horse, one of them must needs content himself with a place behind the other.'

"And again, while recollecting, as we think too keenly, the evils, real or imagined, French Canadians have experienced at British hands, they ought, in justice, to remember the benefits they have experienced from the broad ægis of Britain having been interposed between them and the perils of war and changefulness. For instance, supposing Great Britain had renounced, in the treaty of 1763, the American settlements her arms had gained and her policy secured during that and the three preceding years, would the French colonists of Canada and its dependencies, or those of Louisiana, &c., have fared any the better for it during the godless anarchy of the first French Revolution, or under the iron despotism that succeeded? Let them think of the hideous dramas which were enacted in every other colony, of French origination, between 1789 and 1795. During that space of time—which was a continued national agony for the living generation of Frenchmen—their expatriated relatives found, in Anglicised Canada, a Goshen of peace and security. Their descendants, our worthy fellow-subjects, are proud, and rightly so, that they have preserved, in all their integrity, the religion, habitudes, and pure-mindedness of the early settlers of this noble colony. Let them not forget to whom, under Providence, they owe all that. And, we invite them to mark this well—that the merest fraction of the hundreds of millions of pounds expended by Great Britain in preventing Europe, and finally all Christendom, from becoming a universal despotism—yea, not one penny in the pound of the cost incurred, which even now bends her people almost to the earth, was ever charged against any of her colonies.

"So much for what benefits the men of Britain, if only casually, extended to or secured for the Gallo-American race; and more might justly be advanced, in favor of their generous outlay during times present and not remote, for improving this colony, by canalising its rivers, &c. and enabling native companies to construct public works such as were never undertaken, much less effected, in the dependencies of any nation but that of the truly GREAT Britain.

"Here we pause. We have thought it our duty to adjure one great body of our fellow colonists to join with us, and our common friends over the border, to do honor to all by venerating the memories of the illustrious dead.

" How appropriate to the occasion and place are the inspiring words of the Bard of the Passions :—

> How sleep the brave who sink to rest,
> By all their country's wishes blest!
> When Spring, with dewy fingers cold,
> Returns to deck their hallow'd mould,
> She there shall dress a sweeter sod
> Than Fancy's feet has ever trod.
>
> By fairy hands their knell is rung,
> By forms unseen their dirge is sung.
> There Honor comes, a pilgrim gray,
> To bless the turf that wraps their clay ;
> And Freedom shall awhile repair
> To dwell a weeping hermit there.
>
> COLLINS."

And again, a few weeks afterwards, I copied a most patriotic article approbatory of my proposal in the London *Canadian News* for the then current month, its editor too expressing *his* satisfaction that " the suggestion lately thrown out, of the propriety of holding such a celebration, has been so promptly taken up, both in Canada and America."

But enough, and perhaps too much, said about the organization of a National Tricennium, by the People of British and Federal North America. I now proceed to give a short account of the life and career of my hero, composed of materials derived, for the most part, from sources sealed to the many, and never yet entirely opened even to the few.

————

The family of Wolfe, from which the young general sprang, was of note in the county of Clare, more than two centuries ago. On the capitulation of Limerick, in October 1651, to Ireton the Parliamentarian chief, twenty of the most distinguished of its defenders were excepted from pardon, and reserved for execution. Amongst these were two brothers, George and Francis Wolfe,— the former a military officer, the latter a friar. The friar was hanged, but the captain made his escape. He fled to England (Yorkshire), where he settled. His grandson was Colonel [afterwards General] Edward Wolfe, who distinguished himself under Marlborough, and in the suppression of the Scotch Rebellion of 1715. He commanded the 8th Regiment of Foot.

This Colonel Edward Wolfe was the father of *James*, the subject of the present sketch.

James Wolfe was born on the 2nd January, 1727, at Westerham, in Kent. This pretty little town is situated near the west border of the county, on the declivity of a hill overlooking the romantic stream of the Dart, which rises in the vicinity, and after pursuing a meandering course through a district of much natural beauty, falls into the Thames, below London.

His mother's name was Harriet Thompson.

James was the youngest of two sons, the eldest of whom died in infancy. The house in which the young hero was born was that of the vicar, the Rev. George Lewis, who leased it to the Colonel. Soon after, Colonel Wolfe removed, with his lady and infant son, to a house at the extreme end of the town of Westerham, of very picturesque appearance. It is still standing. Here young Wolfe spent some of his happiest days. It is named, after him—"Quebec House." He attended a private school in the neighbourhood; but it is recorded, that although an ardent and clever boy, he did not in any way distinguish himself, so as to excite remark. Indeed, as will be learned from one of his letters in the Glasgow packet, he received a very imperfect education, and little if any, academic tuition after the age of fifteen.

Destined to the profession of arms, young Wolfe was taken from his studies at that early age, and, on 3d November, 1741, entered his father's regiment as second lieutenant. The period at which he thus became a soldier, was one of uncommon interest in the national history. It was in the interval between two rebellions, when the northern part of the old island, but more especially that section included in the Highlands, was comparatively little known and little cared for. Indeed, of the Scots Highlands it may be truly said, that the greatest ignorance had, till about the year of Wolfe's birth, prevailed. The edge of the ancient animosity be-

'tween the people of the northern and southern divisions of that island, now happily broken and removed, was still keen. The Scottish mind was filled with distrust; it rankled with the remembrance of the treachery which forced on Scotland the then hated Union. The Hanoverian succession was by no means popular in the north; and men's minds fluctuated between the old and the new race of kings.

The Rebellion of 1715, and the prominent part taken in it by the mountain clans, had, however, seriously alarmed the Government of that day, and prompted a more close inspection of Scotland and her warlike hill-tribes. As already said, little was known of the Highlands, beyond that which fatal experience had recently taught, viz., that their dreary recesses were filled with wild and hardy warriors, who held the comparatively peaceful men of the plains in contempt, for cultivating vocations opposed to their own, of clan-strife and war. They were, therefore, ready, on the least signal from their chiefs, to descend with the fury of a mountain tempest on the inhabitants of the Lowlands, and carry devastation around them, with little or no check at the hands of a timid Government.

How curious to read Wolfe's description of a country and a people, *then* nearly as dangerous to visit as once the American wilds, but which is *now* the favourite retreat of royalty itself for recreation from the weight of state cares, and the chosen resort of tourists from every clime!

Such was Scotland in his day; and it was in that country that he wrote the first of the letters to be quoted from. As already stated, he entered the army in 1741, and embarked with his father in the expedition to Flanders, under Lord Cathcart; but being then, and always, of a very delicate constitution, the young soldier became ill, and had to be landed at Portsmouth. After a little while, his health improved; he then joined his father on the Continent, and at once began to learn, practically, the stern lessons of war on the battle field.*

---

* Warburton's *Conquest of Canada*, vol. ii., and *Notes and Queries*.

On 27th March, 1742, young Wolfe was appointed an ensign in the 12th Regiment [Duroure's], and carried the colours at the great battle of Dettingen in that year. In April, 1743, he appears to have been travelling for his health ; and in that month wrote a letter to his mother, still preserved, dated Rome, in a very affectionate and graceful strain.

On the 14th July, 1743, Wolfe was promoted to a lieutenancy in the same regiment, the 12th, commanded by Colonel Scipio Duroure ; and eight days afterwards was appointed adjutant. At that time he was serving with the Allied army, behind the Scheldt.

On 23d June, 1744, he received a captaincy in General Barrel's regiment [the 4th], and served under the Duke of Cumberland, at the bloody and disastrous battle of Fontenoy, fought 11th May, 1745. His bravery attracted the notice of the duke, and he acquired greater distinction than usually falls to the lot of junior officers.

About this period, the second Scotch Rebellion broke out, and several of the regiments serving in Flanders were hastily sent for to aid in its suppression. Barrel's was one of the number, and Wolfe came over with it, in the autumn of that year ; by which time he had received the brevet rank of major.* The troops arrived at Shields and Newcastle in transports, and were speedily marched against the rebels.

Barrel's regiment was hotly engaged at the battle of Falkirk, on 17th January, 1746. General Hawley, who commanded the King's troops at that disastrous conflict, was a veteran aged about sixty-six, and a great favourite of the Duke of Cumberland, but, like him, of coarse and brutal manners, with little military talent. He allowed his army to be surprised in open day, while visiting the Countess of Kilmarnock, and indulging in good cheer, at Callender House. Huske, his second in command, was a good officer, but Hawley allowed him no discretionary power ; other-

---

* This is proved by an order issued by Marshal Wade, dated 2d November, 1745, for " Major James Wolfe to be paid £930, for allowance of 93 baggage horses to the seven battalions *lately* come from Flanders." The original is in the possession of Robert Cole, Esq., London.

wise it is not improbable that Lord George Murray's feint, which threw Hawley off his guard, and principally led to the defeat of the royal army, might have been foiled. When the attack was made by the clans, under cover of broken ground, the king's troops were preparing their dinner; and so deficient were Hawley's arrangements, that although he knew his army was in the immediate vicinity of an energetic foe, he had no pickets or videttes to watch, and give timely notice of the approach of the hostile forces. Some peasants gave the alarm; the drums hastily beat to arms; and a cry arose among the surprised regiments—Where is our general? A mounted officer was sent for him at full speed, with the unexpected and unwelcome intelligence, that his army was attacked. Hawley rushed into the battle without his hat, which was left behind in the drawing-room of Callender House. With his white hair streaming in the storm of wind and sleet, which blew direct in the faces of his soldiers, and favoured by which, the furious broadsword assault had been made on the English regiments, the bewildered general vainly endeavoured to rally his broken and panic-struck battalions. They fled before the clans, with the exception of three regiments, viz., Barrel's, Ligonier's and the Glasgow militia. These bravely stood their ground, and fairly repulsed the attack on that part of the line, besides covering the retreat. Wolfe was in this action; and at the head of his company, in Barrel's foot, behaved with his usual coolness and intrepidity.

In the course of Hawley's retreat to Edinburgh, his dragoons set fire to the fine old Palace of Linlithgow, the favourite residence of several of the Scottish monarchs, and the birth-place of the beautiful and accomplished but much-calumniated Mary Stuart.

Exactly three months after Hawley's defeat, the battle of Culloden was fought, which crushed the Rebellion, and ruined the Pretender's cause.

In this memorable action, Wolfe acted as aid-de-camp to General Hawley with the cavalry. He seems to have preferred this arm of the service to the infantry, and so expresses himself in one of the Glasgow letters, assigning as a reason that he had "good eyes."

It is unnecessary to enlarge on the well-known particulars of the bloody field of Culloden. The rebels fought with desperation. The brunt of the battle fell on the regiments of Barrel and Munro. So furious was the broad-sword charge on these two devoted battalions, that the Highlanders fairly broke through them, and though they defended themselves bravely with their bayonets and spontoons, they would have been cut to pieces, had not Wolfe's father's regiment and another been promptly sent forward from the second line to their assistance, under shelter of which the disordered ranks were re-dressed, and both regiments behaved with great gallantry. Charles Edward lost the day, chiefly through mismanagement, and his own obstinacy. Defeated at all points, the rebels retreated, but in good order; and Cumberland, by no means active in the pursuit, contented himself in the first instance, Russian-like, with murdering the wounded. Though more than one hundred years have passed, the blood so ruthlessly shed by this man-butcher—in humanity's if not reason's ear—still cries from the ground; and his name, deeply dyed as with gore, cannot be mentioned but with abhorrence. Never was there a greater contrast than between Cumberland and his amiable young officer, Wolfe. The latter, brave as a lion, yet kindly in his disposition as a young child; the former the counterpart of a tiger in all its blood-thirstiness and cruelty. Wolfe, a prodigy of military skill; Cumberland, indebted to the accident of being a King's son for a command which tarnished our arms at Fontenoy, outraged humanity in Scotland, and, at a later period, compelled him to retire from the army, a disgrace to his profession, haunted by the ghosts of the murdered old men, the wounded brave, the helpless women and children, ruthlessly cut down by this detestable and well-named "human butcher." A single illustration will show the truth of this contrast. When riding over the field of battle, after the engagement, the Duke observed the young colonel of the Frazer regiment lying wounded. Frazer raised himself on his elbow, and looked at Cumberland, who, offended, turned and said—"Wolfe ! shoot me that Highland scoundrel who thus dares to look on us with so insolent a stare."* Wolfe, horrified at this inhuman order,

* *Vide Brown's Highlands and Clans,* vol. 3, page 251, and authorities there cited.

coolly replied that his commission was at his Royal Highness's disposal, but that he never would consent to become an executioner. Other officers also refusing, a private soldier, at the Duke's command, shot the gallant wounded young officer, Frazer, before his eyes.

After this signal defeat of the rebels, the King's troops were cantoned throughout the disturbed districts to overawe the disaffected. The distribution and quarters of the different regiments during the summer of 1746, are pointed out very distinctly in the *Glasgow Journal* of 31st July in that year, according to which it is ascertained that Barrel's regiment was then stationed at Stirling along with other two; the district general officers there being Major General Bland and Lord Semple. From the battlements of the ancient castle Wolfe often gazed on the magnificent landscape thence unfolded to the spectator. At this time Wolfe was detached with his company to the small fort of Inversnaid, built soon after the rebellion of 1715, at the mouth of the romantic gorge stretching between Loch Lomond and the wild and picturesque region round Loch Ketturin and the Trossachs, to keep the turbulent M'Gregors and Rob Roy in check. This fortified ravine formed the line of demarcation between the countries of the bold M'Gregors, and of the loyal and once numerous clan Buchanan; the upper shores of Loch Lomond skirting the former, and the lower the Buchanans' territory; which last included the lofty broad-shouldered *Ben;* and the group of beautiful, green-wooded islets that stud the bosom of the " Queen of Scottish Lakes," afforded friendly access to the troops, or " red soldiers," sent up from Dumbarton Castle in boats.

The grey ruins of this antique little Inversnaid Fort still linger in peaceful repose. The armed men who there kept ward, and the fiery tribes they were intended to overawe, have alike long passed away; but there *it* stands, as their memorial—its old walls, in some places, kindly screened from the wild mountain blast by the mantling ivy, while the nettle and fox-glove rustle within, as the summer wind plays idly through the ruins.

We can imagine the great-hearted young soldier, surrounded by the grandeur of nature, which must have made a deep impression on his sensitive mind, studying, in this little Highland fortlet, that art which, at no distant day, was to make his name illustrious.

But Wolfe was not allowed to remain long inactive in Scotland. The war on the Continent continued fierce; and several of the best trained and most effective regiments, then in the north, were ordered to Holland, to rejoin the English army, from which they had been the previous year withdrawn by the episode of the Scotch Rebellion. One of these was Barrel's, the discipline of which was considered a model to the whole.

In the campaign which followed, the Allies were commanded by the Duke of Cumberland. But the heartless victor of Culloden had now a very different opponent from Charles Edward. The renowned Marshal Saxe was at the head of the French army, whose great military genius threw completely into shade the pretensions of George the Second's favourite son. Cumberland was incapable of placing an army in a proper position on a field of battle, under the most ordinary circumstances, far less in the presence of such a master of war as then confronted him. The result might have been foreseen. Though the British troops behaved with their usual courage, and performed prodigies of valor, yet being unskilfully posted, their efforts were unavailing. The Duke was fairly out-generalled, and his army repeatedly beaten. This was especially the case at the battle of Laufeldt, in Austrian Flanders, on 2d July, 1747, where Cumberland was totally defeated, and only saved from utter destruction by the indomitable bearing of the British cavalry, under Ligonier, which checked the French advance on the retreating columns of infantry. In this bloody engagement, Wolfe was wounded.* He behaved with great gallantry, and was publicly thanked by the Duke for his conduct. Indeed, he was present at every engagement during the war, and never without distinction. Wolfe also applied himself closely, not only to the improvement of his own military talents,

---

* This is ascertained by the following notice of the wounded, in *Bigg's Military History of Europe*, from 1739 to 1748:—General and Staff Officers:—wounded, Major-Gen. Bland. Majors of brigade, Leslie, Wolfe, Scott, &c.

but to the introduction and maintenance of the most exact discipline in the corps; then generally too little attended to. This he did, without any unnecessary severity. He shewed himself, in all his relations, a good, a brave, an intelligent, and high-minded soldier.

In June, 1748, Wolfe was stationed near Lyon-sur-Meuse, as major of brigade. After the peace of Aix-la-Chapelle, that year, he returned with his regiment to Britain; and was again sent to Scotland.

During the two years which had then elapsed after Culloden, the state of the Highlands had again seriously engaged the attention of Government. A farther glance at that picturesque region will serve to elucidate some of Wolfe's letters.

Accessible though the magnificent Highland country is to the stranger of the present day, it was not, as already said, always so. It was comparatively late in the world's history before the barriers against Lowland intercourse were removed. The Highlanders were jealous of their country being too curiously seen. Warlike, brave, yet turbulent, the Government had little command over them; and schemes of rebellion had been so repeatedly fostered within the dusky glens, followed by outbreaks, that the rest of the country was kept in constant alarm. No proper check existed. The system, too, of armed bands roaming about, stealing, or as they softly termed it, "lifting," whole droves of cattle, and of levying tribute to purchase exemption (called *black-mail*) from that species of robbery, had become intolerable. But when the hopes of the Stuarts were finally crushed at Culloden, the Ministry of George II. determined to put an end to this grievous state of things, and stretch forth the strong arm of British power over the whole Highlands, and compel obedience to the law. Accordingly, a series of very stringent Acts of Parliament were passed in the autumn of 1746, and the year following. By these " rebellion statutes," military tenures, or, in Scottish legal *parlance*, " ward-holdings," were abolished ; the hereditary jurisdictions heretofore wielded by great families, were transferred to the crown ; the clans were to be more effectually disarmed ; the tartan, and all " party-colored dress," was strictly forbidden ; the Scottish Episcopalian clergy (mostly Jacobites) were required, before officiating any longer, to take a prescribed form of oath, abjuring allegiance to the Stuarts, acknowledging King George, and enjoined in the liturgy to pray for him and the Royal family. These enactments were fenced with severe penalties. If arms were found in a Highlander's possession; if he was detected wearing the tartan, or a philibeg; if a priest officiated contrary to the act; or if either refused to take the oaths prescribed, they were liable to six months' imprisonment for the first offence, and transportation to the "American plantations" for the second.

To enforce these acts, a system of military police was established, consisting of parties of the regular soldiers drafted from the principal garrisons in Scotland, and posted throughout the Highlands, with strict orders to compel obedience to the very letter. This soldier-police consisted generally of a captain's guard, stationed at some commanding point of a given district, with a cluster of small subsidiary posts thrown out, in charge of a lieutenant, a serjeant, or a corporal, according to their importance; the intervening distances being under the surveillance of patroles, while parties were frequently sent to scour the mountains. Each small subpost reported to its captain, once a week, all breaches of the law, captures, and anything else extraordinary that had occurred within its sphere; and offenders were handed over, promptly, to the Sheriff of the county. The captains, in their turn, made a report, every fortnight, of all that occurred, both at their own chief stations and their respective subordinate posts, " distinguishing extraordinaries, " to the commander-in-chief of the forces in Scotland at Edinburgh.

Those were severe statutes, probably scarcely justifiable, even on the plea of necessity advanced by those who introduced them. But it was said that milder measures had already failed, and it was hoped that severity would lead to good at last; while a proper direction was sought to be given to the martial habits of the people, by pointing out to them the advantages of enlistment in the king's army. The results are well known; and the now completely altered state of things throughout every corner of the Highlands—where peace, order, and good will to the Government universally prevail, must gratify every true lover of his country.

But one can hardly look back upon the severe period of the Gael's probation, without curiosity and a desire to know something of the working of the military system, which compelled him to abandon his former mode of life and learn new courses. An opportunity has been afforded, by the discovery of an antique manuscript volume of reports, by the various district captains, stationed over the Highlands, to the General, at Edinburgh, during the five years from 31st May, 1752, till 26th September, 1757. This curious volume was lately found at Glasgow, in an old military chest, along with the private parcel of thirteen letters from young Wolfe, already incidentally referred to.* The officer to whom this book belonged, was the same Rickson to whom these letters were addressed. He was attached to the general's staff; and seems to have had charge of the supervision of these military reports.

Now, when Wolfe was sent with his regiment again to the north, in 1748, he found the system of soldier-police in full operation. He did not approve of the troops being dispersed into such small parties all over the Highlands. He preferred large bodies patrolling the country, and thus inspiring greater awe by the aspect of power, than could be expected from mere handfuls of men distant from each other, not easily re-united in case of

---

* Mr. Buchanan, who lent both this book and those letters to me for copying and extracts, a chance by which I largely profited, gave the following account of the finding and bringing of both to the light of day :—

" The discovery was entirely accidental. It happened that an elderly Glasgow gentleman died a few years ago ; in whose possession an antique military-chest had remained more than half a century, uncared for. It was known to have been the property of a relative, long dead—a colonel—but supposed to contain only useless papers. The key had been broken in the rusty lock, and thus the contents were fortunately preserved from dispersion and loss. After the gentleman's death the chest was broken open by his representatives, and found to be filled with antique military reports and papers, besides bundles of old letters. In a corner, carefully tied up by themselves, a group of letters was discovered, bearing the signature *James Wolfe.* By the courtesy of the owner (an old college companion), these letters were placed in my possession."

attack, and liable to be cut off in detail. His views on this subject are seen in letter No. 6 of the series. He gradually condemned
the mode in which the royal troops had been managed during the
Rebellion. In the letter just referred to he writes:—"Such a
succession of errors, and such a strain of ill-behaviour, as the last
Scotch war did produce, can hardly, I believe, be matched in
history. Our future annals will, I hope, be filled with more
stirring events."

On the 5th January, 1749, Wolfe was appointed Major of Lord
George Sackville's regiment [the 20th], and in the month following he was again stationed at Stirling.

He did not long hold the rank of major. He was promoted
lieutenant-colonel of Sackville's on the 20th March, 1749. He
was then stationed with his regiment in Glasgow, and the first
letter of the series is dated from that city, on the 2d of April following. It was in answer to one from his friend, who had con-
gratulated him on his promotion.

Reflecting on his new position as Lieut.-Colonel, at such a
youthful age, he wrote thus:—"I take upon me the difficult duty
of a commander. It is a hard thing to keep the passions within
bounds, where authority and immaturity go together. It is hard
to be a severe disciplinarian, yet humane; to study the temper of
all, and endeavour to please them, and yet be impartial; to discourage vice, at the turbulent age of twenty-three."

Wolfe possessed strong religious sentiment. While in Glasgow
there was no Episcopalian place of worship, and he attended a
Presbyterian Church, probably the Cathedral, the minister of which
was the Rev. Dr. John Hamilton. In a letter to his mother, from
Glasgow, dated 13th August, 1749, he writes—"I have obeyed
your instructions so rigidly that rather than want the Word, I get
the reputation of being a very good Presbyterian, by frequenting
the Kirk of Scotland till our chapel opens."

While Wolfe commanded in Glasgow, he had to call out the
regiment to quell a riot, occasioned by the disinterment of a corpse
by a party of resurrectionists. A great fire having broken out in
the suburb of Gorbals on the night of 5th June, 1749, Wolfe
marched parties of his soldiers to the spot, who assisted in its

suppression, and otherwise were of great service. Upwards of 150 families were burnt out, and great distress ensued among the poor people. Lord George Sackville, and the other officers of the regiment, contributed liberally to the fund subscribed by the citizens for relief of the destitute, and Wolfe was not backward with his purse on this occasion.

In October, 1749, Wolfe marched to Dundee, and in November following he was stationed at Banff, where he appears to have remained till, at least, June 1751, in which month he wrote a letter to his friend Captain Rickson, eleven pages in length, and full of interest. [No. 4.]

By this time his friend had embarked with a division of the army under Cornwallis, for the purpose of settling a strong British colony in Nova Scotia, which had been much neglected. The town of Halifax, fortified with a wooden palisade, began to rise in the wilderness. At that time there was much bickering between the two countries, in regard to the encroachments by France on the British territory, more particularly along the Ohio.

In a letter to his mother, dated Inverness, 6th November, 1751, Wolfe writes—" Where there is most employment, and least vice, there should one most wish to be. I have a turn of mind that favours matrimony prodigiously. I love children, and think them necessary to people in their latter days."

Wolfe remained in the North of Scotland two years longer, viz., till 1753. During that time he appears to have made himself well acquainted with the disturbed Highland districts of Inverness-shire, and the proper military points to be held by troops, including Fort-William, Fort Augustus, and other points along the chain of lakes now forming the Caledonian Canal, and beyond towards the Hebridean sea. He disliked the country very much.

In 1753, Wolfe finally left Scotland, and removed to Reading, where his regiment was reviewed, and highly commended, by the Duke of Cumberland. It was considered one of the best drilled and most efficient battalions then in the service. In December of the same year, he was at Dover Castle; and in the December of 1754, at Exeter, where he seems to have remained till at least March, 1755, as is proved by two of his letters to Rickson, dated from that town. [Letters 5 and 6.]

On 18th February, 1755, (while at Exeter,) he wrote his father thus :—" I find that your bounty and liberality keep pace, as they usually do, with my necessities.   I shall not abuse your kindness, nor receive it unthankfully, and what use I make of it shall be for your honour and the king's service—an employment worthy of the hand that gives it ;" and in writing to his mother, on 28th September in the same year, he says :—" My nature requires some extraordinary events to produce itself.   I want that attention and those assiduous cares that commonly go along with good nature and humanity.   In the common occurrences of life I am not seen to advantage."

From Exeter, Wolfe seems to have marched to Canterbury in the course of the year 1755, and his regiment formed part of the force destined to repel the then threatened French invasion.   In the *Gentleman's Magazine* for 1759, pp. 529–530, the instructions drawn up by him for the guidance of the 20th Foot, should the French effect a landing, appear at full length.   It is an admirable paper; clear, pithy, and comprehensive.   The following are specimens :—" A soldier that takes his musket off his shoulder, and pretends to begin the battle without order, will be put to death that instant.   The cowardice or irregular proceeding of one or two men is enough to put a whole battalion in danger.   A soldier that quits his rank or offers to fly, is to be instantly put to death by the officer who commands the platoon, or by the officer or serjeant in rear of that platoon.   A soldier does not deserve to live who won't fight for his king and country.   There is no necessity for firing very fast; a cool, well-levelled fire, with the pieces carefully loaded, is much more destructive and formidable than the quickest fire in confusion.   All attacks in the night are to be made with bayonets, unless when troops are posted with no other design than to alarm, harass, or fatigue the enemy, by firing at their outposts, or into their camp."—" The death of an officer commanding a company or platoon should be no excuse for the confusion or misbehaviour of that platoon ; for while there is an officer or non-commissioned officer left alive, no man is to abandon his colours and betray his country."

As a war between Britain and France is always possible, occaaionally probable, and, even lately, imminent, it might ere long become useful to reproduce the "Instructions" of 1759, most of the directions in which, stamped with the impress of military genius, would be as suitable now as then. Meantime, I am tempted to cite another article from them, as follows:—

"If the seat of war should be in this strong inclosed country (Kent), it will be managed chiefly by fire, and every inch of ground that is proper for defence disputed with the enemy; in which case, the soldiers will soon perceive the advantage of levelling their pieces properly; and they will likewise discover the use of several evolutions that they will now be at a loss to comprehend. The great facility they have at moving from place to place, and from one enclosure to another (either together or in separate bodies), without confusion and disorder, the easier they will fall upon the enemy with advantage, and retire when it is proper to do so; sometimes to draw the enemy into a dangerous position, at other times to take possession of new places of defence that will be constantly prepared behind them."

When the elder Pitt came into power, in 1756, he resolved, if possible, to remove the stains which various reverses had thrown on our arms, by employing officers of known skill and enterprise, instead of those imbeciles who had been too often in command under former administrations, more particularly that of the Duke of Newcastle. Among the first of Pitt's plans was a descent on the French coast at Rochefort. In this affair Wolfe was employed as quarter-master general. But the warlike minister erred, in not sufficiently defining his plan of operation, and in dividing and frittering the command among no less than *seven* officers. The consequences were what might have been expected. Differences of opinion arose among the commanders, followed by irresolution and fatal delays. Wolfe in vain urged instant and vigorous action. He even landed one night alone on the French shore, and walked two miles up the country! He found there was no real difficulties in the way of debarkation, and that no preparations had been made to oppose it. When he returned to the fleet, he reported the results of his observations; and strongly, but unsuccessfully, urged the generals to land and at once attack Rochefort. He even pledged himself to carry the place, should three ships of

war and 500 men be placed at his disposal. In this he was se-
conded by the gallant young Howe, a naval officer with whom he
had contracted close intimacy as a kindred spirit; but all to no purpose. They were over-ruled by the other five; and, finally, the
enterprise completely failed. The troops returned to England, and
Wolfe and Howe were not backward in expressing their indigna-
tion at the blundering which led to the unsuccessful result.
Wolfe's sentiments on this expedition are expressed in the letter
No. 9, written to his friend after coming home.

Pitt now turned his attention to the French possessions in
North America, and determined to strike a blow there. An expedition was accordingly ordered against Louisbourg, and the principal command was committed to General Amherst, a good officer,
having under him Wolfe and three other brigadiers, with a force
of 13,000 men, and a powerful fleet. The expedition sailed from
England early in 1758. In this important affair Wolfe behaved
with the greatest skill and intrepidity. Louisbourg had a numerous garrison; and the shore, for more than seven miles, was
defended by a chain of posts, with intrenchments and batteries.*
In order to distract the enemy's attention, a false attack was resolved on, to mask the real one which was to be made by Wolfe.
His division consisted of the grenadiers and light infantry of the

---

* Yet, if we may trust to the authenticity of a letter from Wolfe, cited
by Garneau, who calls Louisbourg a mere bicoque, our hero held the
works very cheap :—" Louisbourg (Cape Breton) is a little place, and has
but one casemate in it, hardly big enough to hold the women (referring
to the defensive works) ; our artillery made a havoc among them (the
French garrison), and soon opened (made a breach in) the rampart. In
two days more we should certainly have carried it (by storming). If
this (our) force had been properly arranged, there was an end of the
French colony in North America, in one campaign, for we have, exclu-
sive of seamen and mariners (marines) near to 40,000 men in arms."—
Letter from Colonel (brev. brig.-gen.) Wolfe, to Major James Wolfe, dated July 27, 1758. [The latter I take to be the gentleman thus gazetted
to the appointment mentioned, April 23, 1757 :—" The king has been
pleased to appoint James Wolfe, Esq. to be quarter master and barrack
master general of the kingdom of Ireland, in the room of Lord Forbes."]

army, with Frazer's Highlanders. Before break of day of the 8th
June, the troops were embarked in the boats ; and, while the false
attack was going on under Brigadiers Whitmore and Laurence,
Wolfe's division, under cover of the fire of several frigates and
sloops, dashed boldly towards the shore, through a tremendous
surf, which upset several of the boats, and drowned a number of
soldiers. The landing place was defended by a large body of
French troops, intrenched behind a battery of eight guns. They
reserved their fire till the English came close, when they opened
with great execution. But nothing could resist Wolfe's impetuous
attack. He was the first officer to leap on shore amidst a shower
of bullets, and issued his orders with his usual coolness and pre-
cision. Heading, in person, the light infantry and Highlanders,
he carried everything before him at the point of the bayonet,
pursuing the enemy to the very walls of Louisbourg. The town
was invested ; and, by a series of skilful manœuvres on the part of
Wolfe, he mainly contributed to the final capture of the place.
His conduct throughout this affair was the theme of general
admiration, both in the army and at home, and tended still more
to raise him in the estimation of Mr. Pitt. That able minister
had signified his wish, when conferring on Wolfe the rank of
Brigadier, preparatory to setting out on the Louisbourg expedition,
that, immediately after its termination, he should return to England, instead of remaining with the troops abroad. Wolfe
accordingly did so, and the letter No. 12 was written after his
return. In it, he comments freely on the expedition, and does
not appear to have thought at all favourably of the plan of attack ;
in fact, he says he anticipated a repulse. This letter is the last of
Rickson's packet, and is the more interesting, from being dated only
about two months before his departure again for America, on his
final and memorable campaign against Quebec.

The object of Pitt's wish to have Wolfe back to England was
now made known. He had determined to give him the principal
command in a still more important expedition which he had
planned ; it was to be on a great scale, and to embrace three dis-
tinct objects. The chief part, however, was the capture of Quebec,
the key to the French dominions in Canada. The plan, in all its

parts, was this :—Wolfe, with a large body of troops, and aided by a powerful fleet, was to sail up the St. Lawrence, and besiege Quebec. Amherst, the commander in chief in British America, with 12,000 men, was to attack Ticonderago and Crownpoint (from which we had formerly been repulsed); while General Prideaux was to invest the fort near the Falls of Niagara, commanding the approach to the great lakes. These two last officers, after accomplishing the capture of the places assigned to them, were to find their way to Quebec, and assist Wolfe, the strength of whose division was not considered sufficient by itself to effect the capture of a fortress considered the strongest in America. In short, all the principal French posts were to be attacked at once.

Accordingly, Wolfe left England on the 17th of February, 1759, after having been promoted to the rank of Major-General. Three young brigadiers of talent accompanied him; not a single veteran officer of note being employed. Suffice it to say, that the two portions of the grand plan, under Amherst and Prideaux, were successful, though the latter was killed in the trenches; but difficulties prevented the forces of either from forming a junction with Wolfe. He was, therefore, left alone, with a very inadequate division of troops, not exceeding 8000 men, to undertake the important task assigned to him. Only fancy such an enterprise devolving on a young officer, such as Wolfe was, of thirty-two ! But he was not to be daunted, even by the most formidable difficulties.

Montcalm, a foe all-worthy, was a warrior of middle age, but equally as ardent. The heroic twain were, indeed, of kindred minds, and each felt the other's value as skilful soldiers, while exerting their military talents in the cause of their several fatherlands.*

The fleet which conveyed Wolfe's little army was under Admiral

---

* Louis-Joseph de Montcalm-Gozon, marquis de St. Véran, baron de Gabriac, commander of the order of St. Louis, was born in 1711, and entered the French army at an early age. After serving with distinction in Germany, Italy, &c., he arrived in Canada about mid-May 1756, but with the rank of *maréchal-de-camp* (brigadier-general) only. He afterwards became lieutenant-general and commander-in-chief of the whole forces in Canada.

Saunders. It became necessary to ascertain the soundings of the channel between the island of Orleans and Quebec; and here another young man, whose foot was then only about to ascend the steps of Fame's great temple, distinguished himself. The difficult and dangerous duty of taking the soundings was entrusted to Cook, afterwards so celebrated as a navigator,* destined to explore the vast mysterious oceans of the south and the west, and carry the white man's name and the torch of civilization to the hitherto unknown lands which rear their volcanic peaks, exhibit the wondrous marine architecture of the coral-zoophyte, and shed a delightful tropical fragrance, wafted to the weather-beaten sailor approaching their shores, over the long, broad billows which furrow the blue waste of waters. Cook was then only 31, and acted as master of the Mercury, one of the fleet. He performed the service, for which he had been recommended by Captain Palliser, in a masterly manner, and much to Wolfe's satisfaction, as enabling him the better to mature his plans.

The narrow limits of a lecture quite forbid my entering into details of the siege of Quebec, or of the feats of arms and strategy which preceded, accompanied or followed that event, scarcely making an exception even of the struggle which took place under its walls this day a century ago. Suffice it to say that when a place of landing had been determined upon, and all made ready to effect it by eventide on the 12th day of September, before daylight next morning, though the strength of the current and tide of the river St. Lawrence under the heights of the city carried the boats a little way beyond the point Wolfe† intended, they were brought-to

---

* Through a singular coincidence noticed by M. Garneau, M. Bougainville had yet to become the foremost of his country's navigators, and second only to Britain's most illustrious mariner. But Cook was aided, in piloting, by the French renegade, Denis de Vitré.

† While in the boat, Wolfe, in an under tone, repeated Gray's "Elegy written in a country Church-yard," a poem then in over-repute, and when he had finished, said—"Now, gentlemen, I would rather have been the author of that poem than take Quebec." This anecdote was reported by Professor Robison, of Edinburgh, who was then a young midshipman, and sat near the general.—*Vide Lord Mahon's "England."*

at a place where a narrow pathway, or track, led up, surmounted by a captain's guard. The British soldiers silently sprang on the slippery ledge at the bottom. Not a word or whisper escaped. All knew the value, at this critical moment, of caution ; and none disregarded their favourite General's previous earnest admonitions on this point. Among the very first to land was himself. All knew what they were to perform. The foremost to ascend the dizzy heights was the 87th or Fraser's Highland regiment. Wolfe had often before seen the daring of the kilted soldiers. Slinging their muskets across their backs, they ascended the cliffs with all the agility of Zouaves, using their hands more than their feet ; grasping the projecting wild bushes, and clambering up by the angles on the face of the rock, till they finally reached the summit, where they surprised the officer in command of the French picquet, and a number of the soldiers ; the rest having fled in terror at the unexpected appearance of Scotia's plumes and stalwart sons. The alarm was quickly spread ; but crowds of British soldiers, hastily making their way up the now unguarded narrow pathway before noticed, were instantly formed in battle array, by Wolfe, on the broad plateau, ready to act ; and the key of the position was fairly gained. Several pieces of cannon, in charge of the French guard, had been seized, and some English guns were quickly slung by ropes, and hoisted up to the British position.* By dawn of the memorable 13th of September, 1759, Wolfe's forces stood, ready for action, on the Heights of Abraham.

Montcalm was thunderstruck. He at first refused to believe that the hostile troops could be there ; but, soon convinced of the dread reality, he now saw no alternative, with an English fleet threatening him on one side, and an army opposite his most vulnerable point on the other, than to leave his formidable position, and give battle on the plain. Issuing from the ramparts with the flower of his soldiers, and leaving his field-pieces behind, Montcalm quickly advanced to meet Wolfe, lining the bushes, in front of his position, with picked marksmen, and crowds of Indians, en-

---

* Two of the cannon taken at this point are preserved in the Tower of London. They are remarkably fine brass guns, on carriages.

deavouring, at the same time, to turn the English flank. Heading his old French soldiers, Montcalm came on at bayonet-charge in double-quick time; but Wolfe, desiring his troops to remain firm, and reserve their fire till the enemy came to close quarters, placed himself at the head of the English grenadiers, and, by voice and gesture, encouraged them to complete what had been so promisingly begun. By disease and other casualties, his whole effective force was now reduced to scarcely 5000 men.

The shock of battle came. The British poured in volley after volley, at short distance, with murderous effect. But still the conflict raged. Both armies fought desperately. Wolfe stood conspicuous in the front ranks, giving his orders, and encouraging his men, when a musket-ball hit him in the wrist. Wrapping his handkerchief round the wound, he continued his directions with perfect coolness. He ordered a charge, at the point of the bayonet, on the already wavering French columns, heading it in person, when he received another ball, in the upper part of the abdomen, as he cheered his soldiers on. Even this more serious wound did not for a moment deprive him of his calm self-possession, and he was gallantly leading the charge, when a third and fatal bullet, probably from the same rifle, struck him in the breast, and he fell. It was with difficulty he allowed a party of his grieved soldiers to carry him to the rear. The others, enraged at the fate of their beloved leader, sprang on the enemy, and carried everything before them. Wolfe was fast dying; the crimson streams flowed from the three severe wounds, yet his dimmed eye looked towards the battle, and his ear listened to the shouts of the combatants, the sharp roll of musketry, and the roar of cannon. Extended on the ground, and surrounded by a group of hardy warriors, down whose rugged visages seldom-shed tears trickled, as they hung over *him* who was about to leave them for ever, he anxiously inquired the progress of the engagement. An officer suddenly called out— "They RUN. See, see! *how* they run!" Wolfe, who was in a half-fainting-fit, hearing the exulting shout, eagerly asked—"Who run?" It was answered—"The French; they give way in all directions!" A gleam of satisfaction played for an instant on the dying General's countenance, and he feebly exclaimed—"Then I die content." But these were not literally, as is usually reported, the hero's last words. The latest articulated syllables conveyed an emphatic order for Webb's regiment to move down instantly to the St. Charles River, and secure the bridge there, to cut off the enemy's retreat; after uttering which he expired in the arms of Sergeant Frazer, his favourite orderly.* The next officer in command, Monckton, was dangerously wounded; but the victory was most ably followed up and completed by Townshend, a talented and judicious young brigadier.

Almost at the same time, the brave Montcalm also fell mortally wounded; but he only lived out the day, and expired on the next. With his dying breath he addressed General Townshend, and recommended the French prisoners to "that generous humanity by which the British nation has always been distinguished." His second in command shared the same fate.

In the dispatch sent home by General Townshend, announcing

---

* In one memoir of Wolfe I have seen, it is reported, I know not on what authority, that when he was struck for the third time, anticipating that he could not long survive, he exclaimed, "Support me! let not my brave soldiers see me drop." And turning to a staff-officer near by (name not given) he added, " The day is ours—keep it."

When Wolfe fell, there was found in his pocket a small book—*The Treasury of Fortification*, by John Barker. It is now in the library of the Royal Artillery, Woolwich. On the fly-leaf is a memorandum in the hero's handwriting—" This is an exceeding [good?] book on fortification. —Wolfe."

His sash, saturated with blood, came into the possession of Colonel Stirling, of the 36th Foot, who got it from Sir Samuel Auchmuty.

In the United Service Institution, London, there is a pencil profile of Wolfe, sketched by Harry Smith, one of his aides-de-camp, shortly before the fatal day of battle. It was presented to the Institution by the Duke of Northumberland, when Lord Prudhoe, and hangs near the case containing the sword worn by Wolfe when he fell.

Wolfe's mother wrote three most affecting letters to Pitt, after her son's death, dated 6th, 27th, and 30th November, 1759, which were printed. She survived her husband and son only five years, and died at her house, Greenwich, 26th September, 1764. Her remains were placed beside those she loved so well.

the victory of Sept. 13, the writer did even more honour to himself than to the subject of the following eulogium :—

"I am not ashamed to own to you, that my heart does not exult in the midst of this success : I have lost but a friend in General Wolfe, our country has lost a sure support and a perpetual honour. If the world were sensible at what a dear rate we have purchased Quebec in his death, it would damp the public joy. Our best consolation is, that Providence seemed not to promise that he should long remain amongst us. He was sensible of the weakness of his (bodily) constitution, and crowded into a few years action that would have adorned a length of life."

When the news reached England, the national feeling was one of mingled exultation and sorrow, at the brilliant results on the one hand, and the loss of the gallant Wolfe on the other. Pitt made a most eloquent appeal to Parliament on the complete success of the campaign, and spoke of the transcendent merits of the fallen General, in language which drew tears from all who heard him. He concluded with a motion that an address be presented to his Majesty, praying that he would order a monument to Wolfe's memory in Westminster Abbey. This was unanimously agreed to ; and that ancient edifice, the solemn depository of the undying names of the good and the great, had committed to its charge another marble memorial, recording the worth of him who fell in Britain's cause, covered with glory, and whose name is embalmed in imperishable renown.

Wolfe's father, the brave old General, died only a few days before the arrival of the news ; and the mother of England's young hero had to lament, at one and the same time, in her old age, the double loss of her husband and their only son. Wolfe's body was brought to England, and laid by the side of his father's in a vault of Greenwich parish church.* His military cloak is preserved in the Tower ; and his sword in the United Service Institution, Scotland Yard, London.

---

* I believe the British Government intends to transport Wolfe's remains to Westminster Abbey, and deposit them in the chapel where his monument stands.

Wolfe was to have been married to Miss Lowther, a rich heiress, on his return. Some tolerable, if not affecting lines of poetry were written by him to this young lady on the eve of his departure. The following opening verses form a fair sample of the whole :—

"At length, too soon, dear creature,
　Receive my fond adieu ;
Thy pangs, oh ! love, how bitter,
　The joys, how short, how few !

"I go where glory leads me,
　And dangers point the way ;
Though coward love upbraids me,
　Stern honour bids obey.

"Two passions vainly pleading,
　My beating heart divide ;
Lo ! there my country bleeding,
　And *here* my weeping bride.

"But, ah, thy faithful soldier
　Can true to either prove ;
Fame fires my soul all over,
　While every pulse beats love.

"Then think, where'er I wander,
　The sport of seas and wind,
No distance hearts can sunder
　Whom mutual truth has joined," &c., &c.

Notes and Queries, vol. iv. p. 322.

He gave her a locket with some of his hair. Miss Lowther afterwards became Duchess of Bolton, and always wore Wolfe's last gift, covered with crape. On the arrival of the news of his death, indeed, many persons of all ranks wore mourning in token of respect for him who died in their cause.

————

The narrative part of my self-imposed labour of love is nearly finished. It now only remains for me to give two very brief summaries of the character and deeds of the hero of my story, from two competent estimators, one an eloquent countryman of the great departed, the other an accomplished and great-hearted American writer :—

"Wolfe was assiduously and conscientiously attentive to his profession ; and constitutionally and steadily daring. His mind, clear and active ; his temper lively, and almost impetuous ; independent without pride, and generous without profusion. Great in discipline himself, he was always punctual to obey. His judgment was acute, his memory quick and retentive, and his disposition candid, constant and sincere. The union of the gentle and the bold, of ambition and affection, formed the peculiar charm of his character. His courage never quailed before danger, nor shrank from responsibility. His letters breathe a spirit of gentleness and tenderness, over which ambition could not triumph."*

That name of WOLFE, a household word in the England of a century ago, has even yet a charm in its sound, not only for the ear of every true Briton, but throughout Saxondom on whichever side of the Atlantic it lies. Thus does a popular American historian assure us, that our hero was the especial favourite of his ancestors, and that " his name was long cherished among them with grateful remembrance ;" adding, " how many tears have been shed among us at the simple recital of his death ! How often by the firesides of the colonists, for years afterwards, has the touching ballad, in which his devoted gallantry and his mournful fate are sung, drawn forth the sympathies of the listening circle !" †

Far be it from us, then, to think that these cordial sympathies were wasted on an unworthy object ; for was not our British Bayard " un preux chevalier," alike " sans peur et sans reproche "; gentle as a lamb in the chamber, terrible as a lion in the field !

* Warburton's *Conquest of Canada.* London, 1850.
† History of the United States, ch. 17. By John Frost, Philadelphia. Edit. of 1838.

SUPPLEMENT.

A. — SELECTED PASSAGES FROM WOLFE'S THIRTEEN UNPUBLISHED LETTERS.

LETTER FIRST.

GLASGOW, April 2d, 1749.

Dear Rickson,—When I saw your writing upon the back of a letter, I concluded it was in consequence of the mandate I sent you by Lieut. Herris, of this regiment (that letter he carried upon your account and mine, not his own, as you will easily discover); but I find myself more in your debt than I expected. 'Twas your desire to please, and to express the part you take in your friend's good fortune. These were the motives that persuaded you to do what you knew would be agreeable. You'll believe me, when I tell you that, in my esteem, few of what we call advantages in life would be worth acceptance, if none were to partake them with us. What a wretch is he who lives for himself alone—his only aim! It is the first degree of happiness here below, that the honest, the brave, and estimable part of mankind, or at least some amongst them, share our success. There were several reasons concurring to have sent me into Italy, if this had not happened [promotion] to prevent my intentions. One was to avoid the mortifying circumstance of going, a captain, to Inverness. Disappointed of my sanguine hopes, humbled to an excess, I could not remain in the army and refuse to do the duty of my office while I staid in Britain. Many things, I thought, were, and still are, wanting to my education. Certain never to reap any advantages that way with the regiment; on the contrary, your barren battalion conversation rather blunts the faculties than improves; my youth and vigor bestowed idly in Scotland; my temper daily changed with discontent; and from a man one may become a martinet or a monster.

You shall hear, in justice and in return for your confidence, that I am not less smitten than yourself. The winter we were in London together, I sometimes saw Miss Lawson, the Maid of Honour, General Mordaunt's niece. She pleased me then; but the campaign in view, battledore and dangerous [sic], left little thought for love. The last time I was in town, only three weeks, I was several times with her—sometimes in public, sometimes at her uncle's, and two or three times at her own house. She made a surprising progress in that short time, and won all my affections. Some people reckon her handsome: but I, that am her lover, don't think her a beauty. She has much sweetness of temper, sense enough, and is very civil and engaging in her behaviour. She refused a clergyman with £1300 a-year, and is at present addressed to by a very rich knight, but, to your antagonist's misfortune, he has that of being mad added, so that I hold him cheap. In point of fortune, she has no more than I have a right to expect, viz., £12,000. The maid is tall and thin; about my own age, and that's the only objection. I endeavoured, with the assistance of all the art I am master of, to find out how any serious proposal would be received by Mordaunt and her mother. It did not appear that they would be very averse to such a scheme; but as I am but 22 and 3 months, it is rather early for that sort of project; and if I don't attempt her, somebody else will. The General and Mrs. Wolfe are rather against it, from other more interested views, as they imagine. They have their eye upon one of £30,000. If a company in the Guards is bought for me, or I should be happy enough to purchase any lieut.-colonel's commission within this twelve-month, I shall certainly ask the question; but if I'm kept long here, the fire will be extinguished. Young flames must be constantly fed, or they'll evaporate. I have done with this subject, and do you be silent upon it.

Cornwallis is preparing all things for Nova Scotia; his absence will over-bother me; my stay must be everlasting; and thou know'st, Hal, how I hate compulsion. I'd rather be major upon half-pay, by my soul! These are all new men to me, and many of them but of low mettle. Besides, I am by no means ambitious of command, when that command obliges me to reside far from my own, surrounded either with flatterers or spies, and in a country not at all to my taste. Would to God you had a company in this regiment, that I might at least find some comfort in your conversation. Cornwallis asked to have Loftus with him. The duke [of Cumberland] laughed at the request, and refused him.

You know I am but a very indifferent scholar. When a man leaves his studies at fifteen, he will never be justly called a man of letters. I am endeavouring to repair the damages of my education, and have a person to teach me Latin and the mathematics, two hours in a day, for four or five months. This may help me a little.

LETTER SECOND.

[This letter is dated in 1750, but the place, the outside address and several other parts, are crumbled away. Probably, however, it was still written from Glasgow.]

Dear Rickson,—You were embarked long before I thought you ready for your expedition [to Nova Scotia], and sailed before I could imagine you on board. * * * I look upon his [Lord Cornwallis'] situation as requiring one of his very way of thinking, before all things else; for to settle a new colony, justice, humanity, and disinterestedness are the high requisites; the rest follows from the excellent nature of our Government, which extends itself in full force to its remotest dependency.

In what a state of felicity are our American colonies, compared to those of other nations; and how blessed are the Americans that are in our neighbourhood above those that border upon the French and Spaniards. A free people cannot oppress; but despotism and bigotry, enemies among the most innocent. It is to the eternal honor of the English nation that we have helped to heal the wounds given by the Spaniards to mankind, by their cruelty, pride, and covetousness. Within the influence of our happy Government, all nations are in security. The barrier you are to form, will, if it takes place, strengthen ourselves, protect and support all our adherents; and, as I pretend to have some concern for the general good, and a vast desire to see the propagation of freedom and truth, I am very anxious about the success of this undertaking, and do most sincerely wish that it may have a prosperous issue.

I beg you will tell me at large the condition of your affairs, and what kind of order there is in your community; the notions that prevail; the method of administering justice; the distribution of lands, and their cultivation; the nations that compose the colony, and who are the most numerous; if under military government, how long that is to continue; and what sect in religious affairs is the most prevailing. If ever you advise upon this last subject, *remember to be moderate*. I suppose the Governor has some sort of council, and should be glad to know what it is composed of. The southern colonies will be concerned in this settlement, and have probably sent some able men to assist you with their advice, and with a proper plan of administration. Tell me likewise what climate you live in, and what soil you have to do with; whether the country is mountainous and woody, or plain; if well watered. * * *.

LETTER THIRD.
[Unimportant.]

LETTER FOURTH.

* * You have given me a very satisfactory account of the settlement, as far as you have observed, or have had opportunity to inquire. Till your letter came, I understood that we were lords and proprietors of the north coast of Fundy Bay—for there's a vast tract of country between that and the river of St. Lawrence. It appears to me that Acadia [Nova Scotia] is near an island, and the spot where you are, a very narrow space between the Gulf and Bay. If so, I conclude your post will be greatly improved; and, instead of the shallow works that you describe, something substantial will be erected, capable of containing a large garrison, with inhabitants trained to arms, in expectation of future wars with France, when I foresee great attempts to be made in your neighborhood. When I say thus, I mean in North America. I hope it is true what is mentioned in the newspapers, that a strong naval arma- ment is preparing for your assistance. I wish they would increase your regiment with drafts from the troops here. I could send you some very good little soldiers. If our proposal is a good one, I will shorten the work, and lessen the expense. The present schemes of economy [alluding to the ill-considered views of the Duke of Newcastle's admin- istration] are destructive of great undertakings, narrow in the views, and ruinous in the consequence. I was in the House of Commons this winter, when great sums of money were proposed for you, and granted readily enough, but nothing said of any increase of troops. Mr. Pelham [Secretary of State] spoke very faintly upon the subject; wished gentlemen would well weigh the importance of these undertakings, before they offered them for public approbation, and seemed to intimate that it might probably produce a quarrel with our everlasting and irreconcileable adversary; this I took to be a bad prognostick; a Minis- ter cool in so great an affair, it is enough to freeze up the whole! but perhaps there might be a concealed manoeuvre under these appearances, as, in case of accidents, "I am not to blame," "I was forced to carry it on," and so forth; in the meantime, I hope they are vigorous in support- ing our claims. The country is in all shapes better than we imagined it, and the climate less severe; the extent of our territory, perhaps, won't take a vast deal time to clear; the woods you speak of are, I suppose, to the west of Sheganecto [Schenectady], and within the limits that the French ascribe for themselves, and usurp. Yours is now the dirtiest, as well as the most insignificant and unpleasant branch of military opera- tion; no room for courage and skill to exert itself, no hope of ending it by a decisive blow, and a perpetual danger of assassination; these circum- stances discourage the firmest minds. Brave men, when they see the least room for conquest, think it easy, and generally make it so; but

they grow impatient with perpetual disadvantages. I think Bartloo is a loss; his loggerhead was fit enough for these kind of expeditions, and would save much fatigue to better men. I should imagine that two or three independent Highland companies might be of use ; they are hardy, intrepid, accustomed to a rough country, and no great mischief if they fall. [!] How can you better employ a secret enemy than by making his end conducive to the common good ? If this sentiment should take wind, what an execrable and bloody being should I be considered here in the midst of Popery and Jacobitism, surrounded on every side as I am with this itchy Scots race. [!!] I don't understand what is meant by the wooden forts at Halifax. I have a poor conceit of wooden fortifications, and would wish to have them changed for a rampart of earth, the rest in time ; it is probable that the great attention that must be given at first to building the habitations and clearing the ground about the town, left no interval for other work ; but I hope to hear, in your next letter, that our principal city (Halifax) is considerably improved in strength. You, gentlemen, too, with your parapet three or four feet thick, that a heavy shower would dissolve, you ought to increase it, and put yourselves into a state of security. You appear to be the barrier and bulwark of our settlements on the land, and should be lodged in a sufficient fortress, and with an eye to enterprise. I understand, by your account, that the post you occupy is at a very small distance from the end of the Bay ; and should be glad to know how far that is from the nearest part of the Gulf of St. Lawrence, or from what (in the map) appears to be a lake, or harbour communicating with that Gulf. I rejoice much that you commanded that detachment with which your Lieutenant-Colonel marched; the Indians might have had courage, in that case you would have overcome them in battle under the eye of your chief; as it was, he saw you well disposed to fight—perhaps I am talking at random, but it is conformable to the idea I have of this Colonel *Lawrence*, whose name we often see in the papers. I suppose him to be amongst the first officers of the expedition, high-minded himself, and a judge of it in others; his ready march to the enemy marks the first, and his being the head of your undertaking gives one an opinion of his judgment. If 'tis to his advantage, I desire you to let me have his character at full length; perhaps there's a strong mixture, as it generally happens in ardent men—in that case let's have the best fully, and the other slightly touched. I am mighty sorry that you are not so linked in with some of your brethren as to form an intimacy and confidence; without it, the world is a solitude, and what must your part of it be ? I pity you very heartily, for I am sure you are very ready to mingle with a good disposition. 'Tis doubly a misfortune to be banished without the relief of books, or possibility of reading; the only amends that can be made to us that are sequestered in the lonely and melancholy spots, is that we can fill up part of our time with study. When I am in Scotland I look upon myself as an exile—with respect to the inhabitants I am so, for I dislike 'em much ; 'tis then I pick up my best store, and try to help an indifferent education, and slow faculties, and I can say that I have really acquired more knowledge that way, than in all my former life. I would, by all means, have you get home before the next winter, but I don't approve in the least of the resolution you seem to have taken, rather than continue in that service. Do everything in your power to change, but don't leave the army, as you must, when you go upon half-pay. If there's any female in the case, any reasonable scheme for marriage, I have nothing to say ; that knocks down all my arguments ; they have other sorts of passions to support them * * *. I do think the infancy of a colony has need of able hands, civil and military, to sustain it, and I should be for sacrificing you and all the men of worth, to the general good. You speak of Mr. Brewse, the engineer; pray, say a word or two of his capacity, and tell me if there are, amongst you, any connoisseurs in that business.

Is the Island of St. John [Prince Edward's] in the possession of the French, or do we occupy it ? * * * *

I am not sure whether I mentioned it or not in my last letter, but as 'tis great grief to me, I will hazard the repetition to tell it you. I got powerful people to ask the Duke [Cumberland] no less than three times, for leave to go abroad, and he absolutely refused me that necessary indulgence: this I consider as a very unlucky incident, and very discouraging ; moreover, he accompanied his denial with a speech that leaves no hopes—that a Lieutenant-Colonel was an officer of too high a rank to be allowed to leave his regiment for any considerable time—this is a dreadful mistake, and if obstinately pursued, will disgust a number of good intentions, and preserve that prevailing ignorance of military affairs that has been so fatal to us in all our undertakings, and will be for ever so, unless other measures are pursued. We fall every day lower and lower from our real characters, and are so totally engaged in everything that is minute and trifling, that one would almost imagine the idea of war was extinguished amongst us ; they will hardly allow us to recollect the little service we have seen ; that is to say, the merit of things seems to return into their old channel, and he is the brightest in his profession that is the most impertinent, talks loudest, and knows least * * *.

LETTER FIFTH.

[Unimportant.]

LETTER SIXTH.

* * * Since I began my letter to you, yesterday, there's a fresh and loud report of war. More ships are ordered to be fitted out; and we must expect further preparations, suited to the greatness of the occasion. You in the north [of Scotland] will be now and then alarmed. Such a succession of errors, and such a strain of ill-behaviour as the last Scotch war [the Rebellion of 1745] did produce, can hardly, I believe, be matched in history. Our future annals, will, I hope, be filled with more stirring events.

What if the garrisons of the forts had been under the orders of a prudent resolute man (yourself for instance), would not they have found means to stifle the rebellion in its birth? and might not they have acted more like soldiers and good subjects than it appears they did? What would have been the effects of a sudden march into the middle of that clan who were the first to move? What might have been done by means of hostages of wives and children, or the chiefs themselves? How easy a small body, united, prevents the junction of distant corps; and how favourable the country where you are for such a manœuvre. If notwithstanding all precautions they get together, a body of troops may make a diversion, by laying waste a country that the male inhabitants have left, to prosecute rebellious schemes. How soon must they return to the defence of their property (such as it is) their wives, their children, their houses, and their cattle?

But, above all, the secret, sudden night-march into the midst of them; great patrols of 50, 60, or 100 men each, to terrify them; letters to the chiefs, threatening fire and sword, and certain destruction if they dare to stir; movements that seem mysterious, to keep the enemy's attention upon you, and their fears awake: these and the like, which your experience, reading, and good sense would point out, are means to prevent mischief.

If one was to ask, What preparations were made for the defence of the forts? I believe they would be found very insufficient. There are some things that are absolutely necessary for an obstinate resistance—and such there always should be against rebels—as tools, fascines, turf or sods, arms for the breach (long spontoons or halberds) palisades innumerable; whole trees, converted into that use, stuck in a ditch, to hinder an assault. No one of these articles was thought of, either at Fort Augustus or Fort-George; and, in short, nothing was thought of but how to escape from an enemy most worthy of contempt. One vigorous sortie would have raised the siege of Fort-Augustus; 100 men would have nailed up the battery, or carried the artillery into the castle.

Sergeant M'Pherson* should have a couple of hundred men in his neighbourhood, with orders to massacre the whole clan, if they show the least symptom of rebellion. They are a warlike tribe, and he is a cunning, resolute fellow himself. They should be narrowly watched; and the party there should be well commanded.

Trapaud will have told you that I tried to take hold of that famous man with a very small detachment. I gave the English sergeant orders (in case he should succeed), and was attacked by the clan, with a view to rescue their chief, to kill him instantly, which I concluded would draw on the destruction of the detachment, and furnish me with a sufficient pretext (without waiting for any instructions) to march into their country, *où j'aurais fait main basse, sans miséricorde.* Would you believe that I am so bloody? 'Twas my real intention, and I hope such execution will be done upon the first that revolt, to teach them their duty, and keep the Highlands in awe. They are a people better governed by fear than favour.

My little governor talked to me, some time ago, of a parcel of musketballs that belonged to us, which he offered to send us. We fire bullets continually, and have great need of them; but, as I foresee much difficulty and expense in the removal, I wish he would bestow them, or part, upon you; and let me recommend the practice; you'll soon find the advantage of it. Marksmen are nowhere so necessary as in a mountainous country; besides, firing balls at objects teaches the soldiers to level incomparably, makes the recruits steady, and removes the foolish apprehension that seizes young soldiers when they first load their arms with bullets. We fire, first singly, then by files, 1, 2, 3, or more, then by ranks, and lastly by platoons; and the soldiers see the effects of their shot, especially at a mark, or upon water. We shoot obliquely, and in different situations of ground, from heights downwards, and contrarywise. I use the freedom to mention this to you, not as one prescribing to another, but to a friend who may accept or reject; and because, possibly, it may not have been thought of by your commander, and I have experience of its great utility.

J. W.

Exeter, 7th March, 1755.

---

* Formerly in the "Black Watch," but now a chief of armed *caterans*, and an outlaw. He was afterwards taken and executed. Burns has immortalised him in "Macpherson's Rant."

LETTER SEVENTH.

* * To study the character of your general, to conform to it, and by that means to gain his esteem and confidence, are such judicious measures, that they cannot fail of good effects. If I am not mistaken, Lord George [Beauclerk] is a very even-tempered man, and one that will hearken to a reasonable proposal. If the French resent the affront put upon them by Mr. Boscawen, the war will come on hot and sudden; and they will certainly have an eye to the Highlands. Their friends and allies in that country were of great use to them in the last war. That famous diversion cost us great sums of money and many lives, and left the *Pays-Bas* to Saxe's mercy. I am much of your opinion, that, without a considerable aid of foreign troops, the Highlanders will never stir. I believe their resentments are strong, and the spirit of revenge prevalent amongst them; but the risk is too great without help; however, we ought to be cautious and vigilant. We ought to have good store of meal in the forts to feed the troops in the winter, in case they be wanted; plenty of entrenching tools and hatchets, for making redoubts and cutting palisades, &c.; and we should be cautious not to expose the troops in small parties, dispersed through the Highlands, when there is the least apprehension of a commotion; a few well-chosen posts in the middle of those clans that are the likeliest to rebel, with a force sufficient to entrench and defend themselves, and with positive orders never to surrender to the Highlanders (though ever so numerous), but either to resist in their posts till relieved, or force their way through to the forts, would I think, have lively effects. A hundred soldiers, in my mind, are an overmatch for five hundred of your Highland *milice*; and when they are told so in a proper way, they believe it themselves.

It will be your business to know the exact strength of the rebel clans, and to inquire into the abilities of their leaders, especially of those that are abroad. There are people that can inform you. There ought to be an engineer at the forts to inform the general of what will be wanted for their defence, and to give directions for the construction of small redoubts where the general pleases to order them.

Nobody can say what is to become of us as yet. If troops are sent into Holland, we expect to be amongst the first. We are quartered at Winchester and Southampton; but turned out for the assizes. The fleet at Spithead expects orders to sail every hour. They are commanded by Sir E. Hawke, who has the Admirals Byng and West to assist him. There are about thirty great ships, and some frigates; the finest fleet, I believe, that this nation ever put to sea, and excellently well manned.

JAMES WOLFE.

Lymington, 19th July, 1755.

LETTER EIGHTH.

My dear Rickson,—Though I have matter enough, and pleasure in writing a long letter, yet I must now be short. Your joy upon the occasion of my new employment, I am sure, is very sincere, as is that which I feel when any good thing falls to your share; but this new office does neither please nor flatter me, as you may believe when I tell you that it was offered with the rank of colonel, which the king, guided by the duke [Cumberland], afterwards refused. His royal highness's reasons were plausible; he told the Duke of Bedford (who applied with warmth) that I was so young a lieutenant-colonel, that it could not be done immediately; but I should have known it in time, that I might have excused myself from a very troublesome business, which is quite out of my way. [What does this relate to?] I am glad you succeeded so happily, and got so soon rid of unpleasant guests, and ill to serve; it is ever the case that an unruly collection of raw men are ten times more troublesome than twice as many who know obedience. We are about to undertake something or other at a distance, and I am one of the party. [This relates to the subsequent unlucky descent on Roche-fort.] I can't flatter you with a lively picture of my hopes as to the success of it; the reasons are so strong against us (the English) in whatever we take in hand, that I never expect any great matter; the chiefs, the engineers, and our wretched discipline, are the great and insurmountable obstructions. I doubt yet if there be any fixed plan; we wait for American intelligence, from whence the best is not expected, and shall probably be put into motion by that intelligence. I myself take the chance of a profession little understood, and less liked in this country.

LETTER NINTH.

[This letter was written immediately after Wolfe's return from the unlucky descent on Rochefort.]

Dear Rickson,—I thank you very heartily for your welcome back. I am not sorry that I went, notwithstanding what has happened; one may always pick up something useful from amongst the most fatal errors. I have found out that an admiral should endeavour to run into an enemy's port immediately after he appears before it; that he should anchor the transport ships and frigates as close as can be to the land; that he should reconnoitre and observe it as quick as possible, and lose no time in getting the troops on shore; that previous directions should be given in respect to landing the troops, and a proper disposition made for the boats of all sorts, appointing leaders and fit persons for conducting the different divisions. On the other hand, experience shows me that, in an affair depending upon vigour and despatch, the generals should settle their plan of operations, so that no time may be lost in idle debate and consultations, when the sword should be drawn; that pushing on smartly is the road to success, and more particularly so in an affair of this nature—[a surprise]—that nothing is to be reckoned an obstacle to your undertaking, which is not found really so upon *tryal;* that in war something must be allowed to chance and fortune, seeing it is in its nature hazardous, and an option of difficulties; that the greatness of an object should come under consideration, opposed to the impediments that lie in the way; that the honour of one's country is to have some weight, and that, IN PARTICULAR CIRCUMSTANCES AND TIMES, THE LOSS OF 1000 MEN IS RATHER AN ADVANTAGE TO A NATION THAN OTHERWISE,* seeing that gallant attempts raise its reputation, and make it respectable; whereas the contrary appearances sink the credit of a country, ruin the troops, and create infinite uneasiness and discontent at home. I know not what to say, my dear Rickson, or how to account for our proceedings, unless I own to you that there never was people collected together so unfit for the business they were sent upon—dilatory, ignorant, irresolute, and some grains of a very unmanly quality, and very unsoldier-like or unsailorly like. I have already been too imprudent: I have said too much, and people make me say ten times more than I ever uttered; therefore, repeat nothing out of my letter, nor name my name as the author of any one thing. The whole affair turned upon the impracticability of escalading Rochefort; and the two evidences brought to prove that the ditch was wet (in opposition to the assertions of the chief engineer, who had been in the place), are persons to whom, in my mind, very little credit should be given: without these evidences we must have landed, and must have marched to Rochefort; and it is my opinion that the place would have surrendered, or have been taken in 48 hours. It is certain that there was nothing in all that country to oppose 9000 good Foot—a million of Protestants, upon whom it is necessary to keep a strict eye, so that the garrison could not venture to assemble against us, and no troops except the Militia within any moderate distance of these parts.

Little practice in war, ease and convenience at home, great incomes, and no wants, with no ambition to stir to action, are not the instruments to work a successful war withal; I see no prospect of better deeds; I know not where to look for them, or from whom we may expect them.

---

* I have heard that this sentiment, which I have emphasized typographically having been expressed in conversation almost verbatim as above, and reported to Mr. Pitt, caused that great minister to keep Wolfe in view for some daring enterprise, as soon as opportunity served.

Many handsome things would have been done by the troops had they been permitted to act; as it is, Captain Howe carried off all the honour of this enterprize.

The disaster in North America,* unless the French have driven from their anchors in the harbour of Louisbourg, is of the most fatal kind; whatever diminishes our naval force tends to our ruin and destruction. God forbid that any accident should befall our fleet in the bay!

The King has given me the rank of colonel.   J. W.

Black Heath, 5th Nov., 1757.

LETTER TENTH.

Dear Rickson,—Calcraft told me he had prepared a memorial for you, and was to give it in to Sir John Ligonier. My services in this matter, and my credit with the reigning powers, are not worth your acceptance; but such as they allow it to be, you are as welcome to as any living man. I can assure you that Davy [Colonel David Watson] is double, and would shove you aside to make way for a tenth cousin; it becomes my Lord G. Beauclerk [then Commander-in-Chief in Scotland] to confirm you in your office, by asking and procuring a commission. If he is satisfied with your management, it is his duty to do it; these mealy chiefs give up their just rights, and with them their necessary authority. The Commander in Scotland is the fittest person to recommend, and the best judge of the merits of those that serve under him. Though to all appearance I am in the very centre of business, yet nobody (from the indolent inattention of my temper) knows less of what is going on where I myself am not concerned * * *. Being of the profession of arms, I would seek all occasions to serve; and, therefore, have thrown myself in the way of the American war, though I know that the very passage threatens my life [alluding to his indifferent health], and that my constitution must be utterly ruined and undone; and this from no motive either of avarice or ambition. I expect to embark in about a fortnight.

Black Heath, 12th January, 1757.

[There were "Dowbs" in those days then, as well as Lord Pan-mure's?—B.]

---

* This relates to the capture, by the French, of Fort-William Henry, on the south side of Lake George, with all the artillery, vessels, and boats, on 9th August, 1757, about three months prior to Wolfe's letter. The governor, Monro, had a garrison of 3000 men, and there was a covering army of 4000 besides, under General Webb; but the latter, by the most unpardonable neglect and obstinacy, would not advance to Monro's assistance, who had accordingly to capitulate. Well might Wolfe speak of it as a great "disaster."

LETTER ELEVENTH.

[Written on the eve of sailing from Portsmouth, on the expedition against Louisbourg.]

Dear Rickson,—The title of Brigadier [Pitt had conferred it on him], which extends to America only, has no other advantage than throwing me into service in an easy manner for myself, and such as my constitution really requires; our success alone will determine the more solid favours, for it is possible to deserve very well, and to be extremely ill received. The state of public affairs is such that some measures must be pursued which prudence or military knowledge, perhaps, might not dictate. We shall have (if accident don't prevent it) a great force this year in America, and the country has a right to expect some powerful efforts proportioned to the armaments. Success is in the hands of Providence, but it is in every man's own power to do his part handsomely * * *.

We embark in three or four days. Barré and I have the great apartment of a three-decked ship to revel in; but with all this space and this fresh air, I am sick to death. Time, I suppose, will deliver me from these sufferings; though, in former trials I never could overcome it.

Portsmouth, 7th Feb., 1758.

LETTER TWELFTH.

[Written after Wolfe's return to England, from the capture of Louisbourg.]

My dear Friend,—Your letter dated in September, as well as the last you did me the favour to write, are both received, and with the greatest satisfaction. I do not reckon that we have been fortunate this year in America. Our force was so superior to the enemy's that we might hope for greater success; but it pleased the Disposer of all Things to check our presumption, by permitting Mr. Abercrombie to hurry on that precipitate attack of Ticonderago, in which he failed with loss. By the situation of that fort, by the superiority of our naval force there, and by the strength of our army, which could bear to be weakened by detachments, it seems to me to have been no very difficult matter to have obliged the Marquis de Montcalm to have laid down his arms, and consequently to have given up all Canada. In another circumstance, too, we may be reckoned unlucky. The squadron of men-of-war under de Chafferault failed in their attempt to get into the harbour of Louisbourg, where inevitably they would have shared the fate of those that did, which must have given an irretrievable blow to the marine of France, and delivered Quebec into our hands, if we chose to go up and demand it. Amongst ourselves, be it said, that our attempt to land where we did [alluding to the Louisbourg affair] was rash and injudicious, our success unexpected (by me) and undeserved. There was no prodigious exertion of courage in the affair; an officer and 30 men would have made it impossible to get ashore where we did. Our proceedings in other respects were as slow and tedious as this undertaking was ill-advised and desperate; but this for your private information only. We lost time at the siege, still more after the siege, and blundered from the beginning to end of the campaign. My Lord Howe's death (who was a truly great man) [he was killed in a skirmish in the woods, connected with the repulse of the British in their attack on Ticonderago] left the army upon the continent without life or vigour; this defeat at Ticonderago seemed to stupify us that were at Louisbourg; if we had taken the first hint of that repulse, and sent early and powerful succours, things would have taken perhaps a different turn in those parts before the end of October. I expect every day to hear that some fresh attempts have been made at Ticonderago, and I can't flatter myself that they have succeeded; not from any high idea of the Marquis de Montcalm's abilities, but from the very poor opinion of our own. You have obliged me much with this little sketch of that important spot; till now I have been but ill acquainted with it.

Broadstreet's *coup* was masterly.* He is a very extraordinary man; and if such an excellent officer as the late Lord Howe had the use of Broadstreet's uncommon diligence and activity, and unparalleled batoe knowledge, it would turn to a good public account. When I went from hence, Lord Ligonier told me that I was to return at the end of the campaign; but I have learned since I came home, that an order is gone to keep me there; and I have this day signified to Mr. Pitt that he may dispose of my slight carcase as he pleases, and that I am ready for any undertaking within the reach and compass of my skill and cunning. I am in a very bad condition both with the gravel and rheumatism, but I had much rather die than decline any kind of service that offers; if I followed my own taste, it would lead me into Germany, and if my poor

* This refers to the surprise and capture of the important French fort, Frontinac, on the north or French side of the St. Lawrence, where it issues from Lake Ontario, by Lieut.-Colonel Broadstreet, who had been sent against it by General Abercrombie, with a detachment of 3000 Provincials. This able officer destroyed the fort, with 60 pieces of cannon, 16 mortars, an immense depot of provisions for the French army; took all the enemy's shipping on the lake, consisting of nine vessels, some of them mounting 18 guns, and rejoined Abercrombie, all without the loss of a man. Wolfe's compliment to him was well merited.

talent was consulted, they should place me in the cavalry, because nature has given me good eyes, and a warmth of temper to follow the first impressions. However, it is not our part to choose, but to obey.

My opinion is, that I shall join the army in America, where, if fortune favours our force and best endeavours, we may hope to triumph.

I have said more than enough of myself; it is time to turn a little to your affairs; nothing more unjust than the great rank lately thrown away upon little men, and the good servants of the state neglected. * *

JAMES WOLFE.

Salisbury, 1st December, 1758.

Remember that I am Brigadier in America, and Colonel in Europe.

Barré was in such favour with General Amherst that he took him to the Continent, and he very well deserves his esteem.

LETTER THIRTEENTH.

[A fragment is all that remains. From circumstances, there is a presumption that the fragment was written about the time Wolfe was stationed at Canterbury, in 1755. The object in writing the letter was to give a young officer, who had just entered the army, some good practical advice how to become a thorough soldier.]

Dear Huty,—By a letter from my mother I find you are now an officer in Lord Chs. Hay's regiment, which I heartily give you joy of; and as I sincerely wish you success in life, you will give me leave to give you a few hints, which may be of use to you in it. The field you are going into is quite new to you, but may be trod very safely, and soon made known to you, if you only get into it by the proper entrance.

I make no doubt but you have entirely laid aside the boy, and all boyish amusements, and have considered yourself as a young man going into a manly profession, where you must be answerable for your own conduct. Your character in life must be that of a soldier and a gentleman: the first is to be acquired by application and attendance on your duty; the second by adhering most strictly to the dictates of honour, and the rules of good-breeding. To be more particular on each of these points: When you join your regiment, if there are any officers' guard mounted, be sure constantly to attend the parade, observe carefully the manner of the officers taking their posts, the exercise of their spontoons [short pikes], &c.; when the guard is off from the parade, attend it to the place of relief, and observe the manner and form of relieving; and when you return to your chamber (which should be as soon as you could, lest what you saw slip out of your memory), consult *Bland's Military Discipline* on that head; this will be the readiest method of learning this part of your duty, which is what you will be the soonest called on to perform.

When off duty, get a sergeant or a corporal, whom the adjutant will recommend to you, to teach you the exercise of the firelock, which I beg of you to make yourself as much master of, as if you were a simple soldier; the exact and nice knowledge of this will readily bring you to understand all other parts of your duty, make you a proper judge of the performance of the men, and qualify you for the post of an Adjutant, and, in time, many other employments of credit. When you are posted to your company, take care that the sergeants and corporals constantly bring you the orders; treat those officers with kindness, but keep them at a distance, so will you be beloved and respected by them; read your orders with attention, and if anything in particular concerns yourself, put it down in your memorandum book, which I would have you keep constantly in your pocket, ready for any remarks; be sure to attend constantly morning and evening the roll calling of the company, watch carefully the absentees, and inquire into reasons for their being so, and particularly be watchful they do not endeavour to impose on you sham excuses, which they are apt to do with young officers, but will be deterred from it by a proper severity in detecting them * * *.

Such are the chief parts of the packet of Wolfe's letters.* Fragmentary though they be, they are valuable, for so little is known of his personal history, that even a slight accession is interesting, and worthy of preservation. These letters open up glimpses of his character, and exhibit the tone and bent of his mind, through a medium very favourable for enabling us to judge. Written frankly and unreservedly, to one he sincerely esteemed, we gain access to his inmost thoughts and opinions on subjects both of public and private interest; while we cannot fail to admire the warm and disinterested friendship evinced throughout—the proofs of a generous heart; and we rise from the perusal with renewed regret for the early fall, and increased respect for the memory, of one in all respects so estimable and so worthy of the renown inseparable from his name.

---

* Another letter by Wolfe, pointing out the best military books for a young officer to read, may be seen in the *Edinburgh Magazine* for January, 1852; and a few more first met the public eye in a Montreal daily paper, some five years ago.

B.

Notice of the Commemoration of "The Second Battle of the
Plains of Abraham" (so called by M. Garneau), fought in 1760,
translated from a number of *l'Illustration*, or "Illustrated News"
of Paris, published July 31, 1854 :—

"On the 5th day of June last, there was celebrated at Quebec, the
commemoration of the removal of the remains of the Franco-Canadian
and British soldiery and militia killed in battle August 28, 1760, under
the walls of Quebec; upon which occasion, the French, commanded by
the Chevalier de Levis, gained a signal victory over General Murray,
Governor of Quebec, and Commander-in-chief for England in Canada.
Upon this occasion, the bones of the conquerors and the vanquished,
having been previously raised from the spot, where they had reposed
indiscriminately together for nearly a century, were borne in procession
to a new and more honourable place of sepulture, with great pomp and
solemn observance."

After giving many details of the proceedings, the writer, quoting
the *Journal de Quebec* as his authority, thus proceeds :—

"The corners of the funeral car were supported by Messrs. Morin,
Taché, Caron, Laterriere, Chabot, Chauveau, Salaberry, Panet, Viger,
Cauchon, Garneau, Faribault, Legaré, Dumoulin, Baillargé, and Deputy-
Adjutant-General Macdonald. The British soldiers of the 66th and 71st
Regiments of Foot rendered military honours to the victorious bones of
the French departed, at an auspicious moment; namely, at an epoch
when Britain and France, in armed brotherhood, were battling together
for a common cause upon a soil of the olden world [adverting to the
campaign of the Crimea and siege of Sebastopol.] Arrived at Govern-
ment-house, M. Louis Panet made an harangue to the Governor of
Quebec; who made a suitable reply thereto, in course of which he con-
gratulated the citizens and others present upon the becoming manner
in which the happy idea of honouring the relics of the brave of other
days had been carried out. Thereafter Colonel Taché, in an historical
discourse, which lasted one hour, described the battle in which his forefathers triumphed. Prolonged cheers followed, not unaccompanied
with *hurrahs* for success to the arms of the Allies against those of Rus-
sia," &c.

" Now," demanded the sympathising writer for *l'Illustration*, " was there nothing in all this, than every-day complimentary ceremonials? Not to speak of the visible signs therein of a consoling sympathy between the men of alien race and adverse creeds, long bitterly discordant, and even in our own day at open war, we derive an assurance that England and France, in cordial union now and for ever, as having common objects in view, will, between them, rule the whole civilised earth. *Transit figura hujus mundi:* the alliances of empires, indeed, are subject to change; man himself passes away; but the spirit of religion and the sentiment of human benevolence are eternal."

Nor does it appear that the Quebec Demonstration gave the smallest offence to the British-descended portion of the citizens, or to the English-speaking population of any other part of the Canadas. Why, then, should the French journalists of the Province have taken such strong exception in 1858-9 (only four or five years afterwards) to a proposition of a like nature—if of more comprehensive character—proposed to be carried out at the present time, to do honour alike to our several ancestors, British and French—those who fought and bled to conquer, those who fought and died in vain? Are Britain's fairly-gained successes never to be *pardoned?* " We pause for a reply."

Meantime, let all Canadians of French descent be assured that WE, men of British origin, indorse, generally, this sentiment of the great Lord Chatham, who stimulated the conquest of Canada : " I have ever loved HONOURABLE WAR"—it is not in Anglo-Saxon nature to practise any other. We always respected and yet respect the memory of the dead, of both races, who lay, side by side, stark and cold, on the Plains of Abraham, this day a completed century ago. Adopting, modifiedly, the words of an eminently patriotic poet to my own use, I thus conclude :—

> " True Britons ex~~lt not o'er those they've laid low,
> Whose back's on the field, and their feet to the foe;
> Who losing the battle, unblotted their name,
> Look proudly to heaven from the death-bed of Fame."

A. B.

3 MONTCALM STREET, MONTREAL,
    September 13, 1859.

THE END.